That Bird on My Plate

Written by
Marianne Hesse

Illustrated by
Angela Paul

LUMINARE PRESS
WWW.LUMINAREPRESS.COM

That Bird on My Plate
Copyright © 2021 by Marianne Hesse

All rights reserved. This book or any portion thereof may not be reproduced or used in any manner whatsoever without the express written permission of the publisher, except for the use of brief quotations in a book review.

Printed in the United States of America

Illustrations by Angela Paul
Graphic design by Claire Flint Last

Luminare Press
442 Charnelton St.
Eugene, OR 97401
www.luminarepress.com

LCCN: 2021918130
ISBN: 978-1-64388-797-5

*For Andrew,
who could have easily given
Freddie a run for his money;
and for Tristan,
just because.
—Marianne Hesse*

*To George,
for always being there for me
and for being the most amazing
person in my life.
I love you.
—Angela Paul*

Come on, dear Freddie, please finish your plate
You've dawdled, time's dwindled, and now it's quite late

Toys need to be picked up, your bath must be drawn
So hurry, dear Freddie, don't sit there till dawn

Mummy, if I do not hurry and eat
Don't think for one moment that I have cold feet
A creature with features too dark to relate
Is sharpening his claws as he's eyeing my plate

His wingspan is frightening, his feathers are brown
Fearsome black eyes and a rapt hawkish frown
You know I'm not one to complain, mope or whine
But he's glaring at me like it's his food, not mine!

Whatever I do, I'd best be polite
Perhaps he will go if I give him a bite
Now he's hopped on my plate and he's eating the fish
Who knew he'd be partial to your favorite dish
He's nibbling the beets and the brussels sprouts too
So tell me, dear Mummy, what am I to do?

That bird on my plate mashed my food with his feet
Do you still want me to hurry and eat?
He's dipping his beak in my clear consommé
And the last thing he's doing is going away!

He's got me confused, I don't know what to think
He's perched on my glass, now he's taking a drink
Though the milk might be curdled, I doubt that he cares
This might be my one chance to run up the stairs

This might be my one chance, I may not get two
So tell me, dear Mummy, what am I to do?

Freddie, dear Freddie, what more can I say
Than run when you're ready, run quickly away
Rush straight to your room, then slam the door tight
Once safely inside, son, go turn on the light

Catch your breath for a moment, give your head time to clear
I bet, before you know it, you'll forget he's been here
Look over by the nightstand, you'll see I left the broom
When you're no longer shaken, you can start to clean your room

Put your toys in the toy box, get your shoes off the chair
How often have I told you you're not to leave them there?
Put your books on the shelf and do not sit down to play
The clock continues ticking, so hop to it right away

Mummy, you know I'm not one to talk back
And to please you, I'd toil till the skies turned quite black
But a bear's in my bedroom and he won't let me clean
He's snorting and snarling and I fear he'll turn mean

If that bear hadn't shown up to ruin things, mum
My room would be spotless, you'd not find a crumb
A lump or a crease or a sticky gum drop
I'd work through the night till you told me to stop

But the bear in my bedroom is glaring at me
And I fear if I try to clean up the debris
He might swat at my face, wrestle me for the broom
Then use it to bat your poor boy round the room

Oh no, now he's drooling on my teddy bear!
From the way that he's growling, I don't think he'll share
My toys are all scattered, I'm sorry to say
But the bear in my room seems to like it that way

If only I could, I would send that rogue packing
I've had quite enough of his boorish ransacking

But what if his snout gets stretched into a snit?
This could be a bear on the cusp of a fit!

To be on the safe side, I'd best keep quite still
I don't want to end up as grist for his mill

I'm sure if we're patient, he'll tire of his play
And then, once he's gone, I'll put all my things away

Freddie, get ready to tiptoe from your room
You've no need to worry, don't fret, fuss or fume
Bears have poor eyesight, I heard that somewhere
So when his head is turned, simply scurry out of there

Tiptoe to the bathroom, then quickly lock the door
Put your clothes in the hamper, don't throw them on the floor
Once you're in the tub, please make sure you wash your hair
And Freddie, don't splash and leave puddles everywhere!

Mummy, I wish I could do as you ask
A soak in the tub would be such a sweet task
Considering all that I've just been put through
I can't think of anything I'd rather do

But the tub isn't empty I'm sorry to say
And whatever's inside seems determined to stay
I'm tongue tied and trembling and I guarantee
If you stood where I stand, you'd be shaking like me

That thing in my bathtub is both big and gray
And the last thing it's doing is going away!
On closer inspection, I fear it might be
A whale or a shark or a stout manatee

I'm almost convinced it's no shark or a whale
I think if it were, it would not wag its tail
I'm still not quite sure I can trust my own eyes
This manatee, mum, is humongous in size!

Although he seems gentle and has a sweet face
He's still taking up every last inch of space
It's quite a tight squeeze for that big old sea cow
The tub would run over if I got in now

Mummy, I think the best thing I can do
Is just wait my turn till the manatee's through
I promise I'll scrub all my fingers and toes
I'll do it the moment that manatee goes

Freddie, dear Freddie, of course you must wait
To pick up your toys, take a bath, clean your plate
You must be exhausted, you've had quite a night
So hop into bed, dear, and turn off the light

Mummy, tell me I did not hear you right
Go to bed with no story, no last kiss goodnight?
You know I can't sleep till you've tucked me in tight
So why would you say I should turn off the light?

Freddie, I trust you'd be first to suggest
That I be polite though I'm somewhat hard pressed

A hairy black ape with a dagger and cape
Is dousing himself with cologne
Though he's somewhat uncouth, he's a sweet snaggletooth
And he should not be left on his own

I'm certain, in time, he will tire of his play
By morning's pale light, he might wander away
As soon as he leaves, son, I'll come say goodnight
Now hop into bed, dear, and turn off the light.

About the Author
Marianne Hesse

That Bird on My Plate is the author's second children's picture book. Her first, *Then We'll Say Goodnight* was also done in collaboration with illustrator, Angela Paul, and, in both instances, animals played a prominent role. While some animals might take umbrage at such a portrayal, no impertinence was ever intended.

About the Illustrator
Angela Paul

Angela Paul is a character artist and illustrator from Germany. Her first children's book illustration was for *Then We'll Say Goodnight.* She is currently studying animation and games.

Made in the USA
Las Vegas, NV
11 April 2022